LET'S HAVE FUN
with Elmo and Friends!

Storybook Treasury

Dalmatian Press, LLC, 2009. All rights reserved.
Published by Dalmatian Press, LLC, 2009. The DALMATIAN PRESS name and logo
are trademarks of Dalmatian Press, LLC, Franklin, Tennessee 37067. 1-866-418-2572
No part of this book may be reproduced or copied in any form
without written permission from the copyright owner.

Printed in China
ISBN: 1-40375-815-8

09 10 11 12 CTP 34398 10 9 8 7 6 5 4 3 2 1
18382

By P.J. Shaw • Illustrated by Tom Brannon

D
Dog

Cowabunga!

Hey, diddle-diddle,
The cat and the fiddle,
The cow jumped over the *moooooon.*
The little dog laughed to see such sport,
And the dish ran away with the spoon.

H House

I Ice Cream

Have some ice cream, Hansel— on the house!

How inviting!

It's Heavenly Honey! Hansel's favorite.

J

Jack

Jog and juggle! Jack, be quick!
Jack, jump over the candlestick!

Enough jogging, juggling, and jumping. I, Jack, am going back to beanstalks.

L
Lamb

Prairie had a little lamb,
Little lamb, little lamb.
Prairie had a little lamb.
Its fleece was light as snow.

Pat a pie, pat a pie, baker's man.
Make me a pie as fast as you can.
Pat it and prick it and mark it with **P**.
Put it in the oven for piggy and me!

The End

S is for School!

By P.J. Shaw • Illustrated by Joe Mathieu

Hello, Dorothy!
Today was Elmo's
first day of school.
What's that, Dorothy?
You want to know
what it's like on
the very first day
of school? Elmo
will tell you.

The first day of school is *so* exciting!

Just getting there is an adventure!

Some monsters wonder what to do on the first day of school.

At school, you might feel a little lonely now and then.

But a smile helps you make new friends. A smile—and some crayons!

On the first day of school, a little fish can get homesick... so bring a picture for company. Guess what? Elmo brings a picture of Dorothy!

On the first day of school you see lots of new faces.

Lots of *friendly* faces! Yay!

The *end* of the first day of school is exciting, too.

It's a good time
for sharing what you've learned…

...with a friend!

The End

What Makes You Giggle?

By P.J. Shaw • Illustrated by Tom Brannon

What makes you giggle,
What gives you a grin?
Big Bird in a tutu doing a spin!

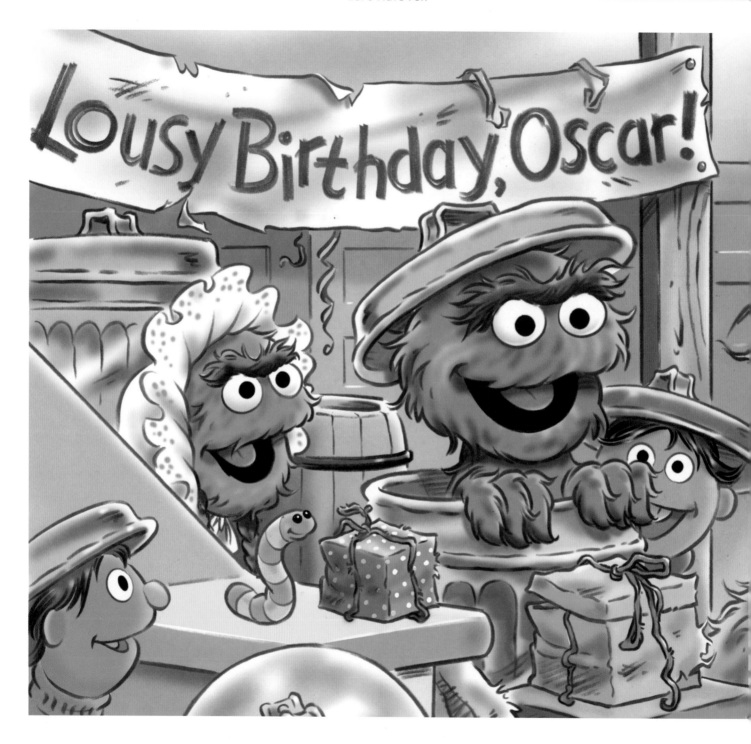

What makes you chuckle,
Or tickles your tummy?
A grouch birthday party—
Where presents are crummy!

Do giraffes give you laughs
On a trip to the zoo?
Or how about chimps?
Monkey-see, monkey-do!

A Snuffleupagus race
Might just give you a smile.
They *galumph* to the finish.
Alice wins by a mile!

What makes you laugh,
What makes you giggle?
A monstrous contest
For noses that wiggle!

Halloween's fun...
And so spooky, you shriek!

GO AWAY

Hide-and-seek, trick-or-treat,
Oscar's can—EEK!

What makes you whoop,
Makes you squeal with delight?
A day at the pool,
When the water's just right.

LIFEGUARD ON DUTY

Dive rings and water wings,
Snorkels and masks.
Flippers and floaties,
And fountains that splash!

What makes you snicker,
Guffaw or tee-hee?
A neighborhood cookout
At Nani Bird's tree?

Make-your-own cupcakes
With milk-chocolate chips?
Maybe strawberries, raisins,
Or cinnamon bits....

Coconut, sprinkles,
Or butterscotch drops,
And pink-and-white frosting
To plop right on top.

What makes you goofy?
What makes you titter?
To trade silly faces
With Curly Bear's sitter!

A Twiddlebugs' picnic
With muffins and honey?

Or...an all-Grover rodeo—
Now, *that* would be funny!

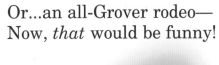

What makes you giggle—
Makes you feel really good?
Just a regular day,
In your own neighborhood!

The End

ABBY CADABBY'S
Rhyme Time

By P.J. Shaw • Illustrated by Tom Leigh

"Lumpkin, bumpkin, diddle-diddle dumpkin, zumpkin, frumpkin, pumpkin!

As a fairy-in-training, I practice my magic tricks with rhymes— you know, words that end with the same sound, like **bat** and **cat**! Rhymes are so fun to find! I know—let's find some rhymes together. Hmmmm. What words rhyme with … **rhyme**?"

What words rhyme with **sheep**?
Noisy cars that go "**beep**"!
A ballet dancer's **leap**,
And a trash heap to **sweep**.

What words rhyme with **go**?
I bet that you **know**!
There's a boat you can **row**,
And cars that go *slooooow*.

What rhymes with **icky**?
Bubblegum that is **sticky**,
A game that is **tricky**,
And dogs who are **licky**.

Which words sound like **zap**?
Fairy wings going **flap**!
And the shoes that you **tap**
To the beat—as you **snap**!

Do some words rhyme with **stick**?
Yes! A house made of **brick**,
A soft baby **chick**,
Or a camera to **click**!

What rhymes with **nose**?
Snuffleupagus **toes**,
A swishy fish that **glows**!
And a slithery **hose**.

What words rhyme with **sloppy**,
Like Oscar's **Jalopy**?
Bunnies all **hoppy**
With ears that are **floppy**.

And last, what rhymes with **tabby**?
A blankie that's **shabby**,
A fairy named **Abby**,
And the family **Cadabby**!

The End

The Penguin

Adapted from the script by Luis Santeiro

"Well, Bert, here we are in Antarctica," said Ernie. "Land of ice and snow and . . . *brrrrr* . . . cold!"

"Don't forget penguins," said Bert. "My favorite birds—after pigeons, of course."

"Of course."

Just then. . .

Plip-plop-plip-plop! A small penguin waddled past them.

"Oh! Oh, look at that!" said Bert. "Follow that penguin!"

So they did! *Plip-plop-plip-plop!* went the penguin. *Plip-plop-plip-plop!* waddled Bert and Ernie.

"Uh, Ernie," mumbled Bert, "I love penguins, but why are we walking like one?"

" 'Cause, Bert," answered Ernie, "this wobble-waddle keeps you pretty warm."

Suddenly, the penguin stopped and began to wiggle-waggle.

"What's he doing?" whispered Ernie.

"I think it's a *she*," said Bert. "And . . . could it be??"

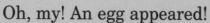

Oh, my! An egg appeared!

"It *is*!" cried Bert, leaning closer. "She's going to be a mama penguin! She's hatching an egg! Uh-oh!"

Fwip! The penguin took hold of Bert's parka and—*fwop!*—plopped him right on top of that egg, with a *squawk-squawk-chirp-squawk*.

"Looks like now *you're* hatching it, Bert. Hee hee hee!" snickered Ernie. "And she thinks you speak penguin."

"Sorry," Bert told the penguin. "I only speak a little pigeon. *Ah, coo-coo, coo-coo-coo.*"

But the penguin turned and dove through a hole in the ice. "Now what?" said Ernie.

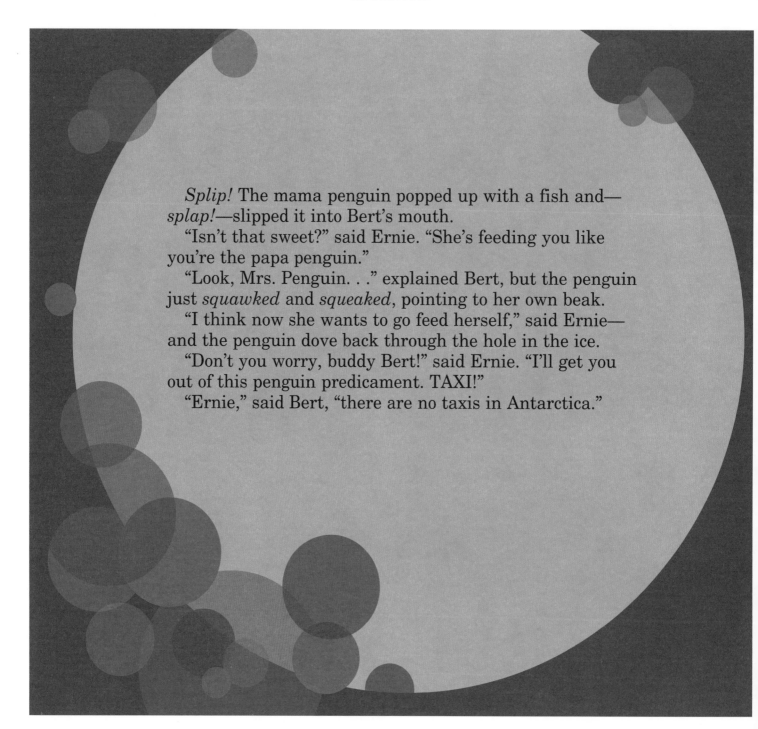

Splip! The mama penguin popped up with a fish and—*splap!*—slipped it into Bert's mouth.

"Isn't that sweet?" said Ernie. "She's feeding you like you're the papa penguin."

"Look, Mrs. Penguin. . ." explained Bert, but the penguin just *squawked* and *squeaked*, pointing to her own beak.

"I think now she wants to go feed herself," said Ernie—and the penguin dove back through the hole in the ice.

"Don't you worry, buddy Bert!" said Ernie. "I'll get you out of this penguin predicament. TAXI!"

"Ernie," said Bert, "there are no taxis in Antarctica."

"Hee hee hee! But there are *dogs* named Taxi!" chuckled Ernie, as a sled dog ran up. "Good boy, Taxi! Come on, Bert! Let's get out of here."

"Wait!" said Bert. "We can't leave this egg. Someone has to keep it warm, or it won't hatch. This egg is . . . Ernie . . . Where's the egg?"

"Oh, no!" cried Bert as they watched Taxi sniff at the egg, pushing it toward—and right over—a cliff!

"Follow that egg!" called Ernie.

Bert and Ernie hopped onto the sled. *Zoom!* They were off, following that egg!

Meanwhile, Mama Penguin popped back up onto the ice with another fish. She waddled happily in search of "Papa Penguin" Bert. But, where was Papa Penguin? And—*squawk!*—where was Mama Penguin's precious egg?

She looked around.

There were sled tracks in the snow.

Plip-plop-plip-plop-wobble-waddle-plip-plop.

She followed those tracks.

"Whew! I'm so glad we caught up with this egg!" said Bert. "Mama Penguin must be worried sick wondering where it is."

"Would you look at Taxi!" chuckled Ernie. "Making snow angels! I think I'll make one, too! Hoo-hoo!"

"Ernie. . ." said Bert as Ernie dove into the snowbank with Taxi. "Ahem! Ernie. . ."

"Stop worrying, Bert. Mama Penguin will find us. She'll be here any minute."

Bert looked down at the egg with a sigh. "Boy, it sure takes patience to be a papa penguin."

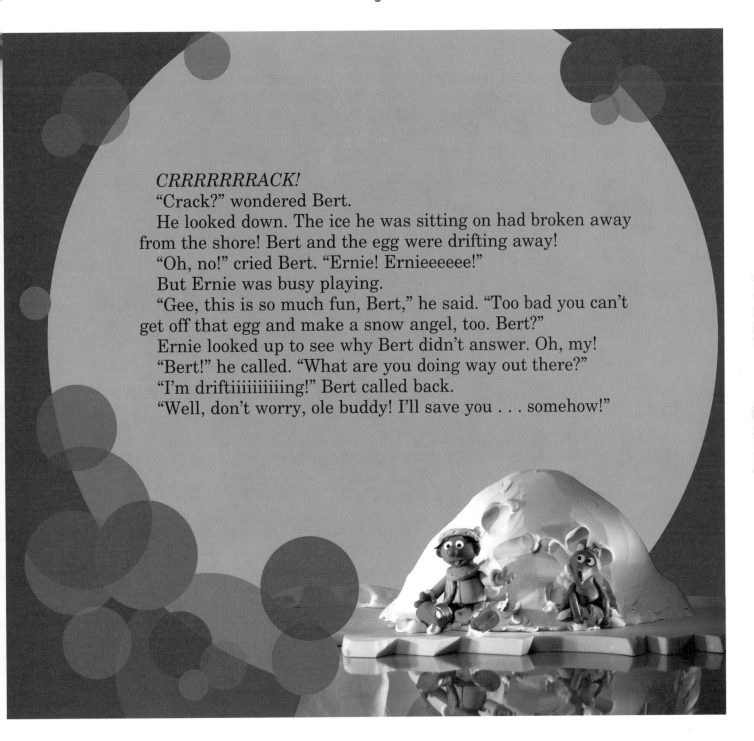

CRRRRRRRACK!

"Crack?" wondered Bert.

He looked down. The ice he was sitting on had broken away from the shore! Bert and the egg were drifting away!

"Oh, no!" cried Bert. "Ernie! Ernieeeeee!"

But Ernie was busy playing.

"Gee, this is so much fun, Bert," he said. "Too bad you can't get off that egg and make a snow angel, too. Bert?"

Ernie looked up to see why Bert didn't answer. Oh, my!

"Bert!" he called. "What are you doing way out there?"

"I'm driftiiiiiiiiiing!" Bert called back.

"Well, don't worry, ole buddy! I'll save you . . . somehow!"

Plip, plop, plip, plop! Squawk, squawk.

Mama Penguin waddled from around the corner. She looked to the right. She looked to the left. She looked up at Ernie. *Squawk?*

Ernie pointed out to the water.

"It's out there," he said, "with Papa."

SQUAWK!!

Ernie looked at the harness and dog reins. He looked at Mama Penguin.

"Well, here," he said, slipping the harness over her head. "Maybe you can use this."

Ga, ga, gaaa!

With the reins trailing behind her, Mama Penguin swam out to the floating ice. Bert grabbed hold of the reins and—*hooray!*—Mama Penguin pulled Bert and the egg back to shore.

"Bert!" cheered Ernie, giving him a big hug. "You're safe!"

"Arf! Arf!" agreed Taxi. "Arf! Arf! Arf!"

Bert gave Mama Penguin a big hug.

"Thank you! Thank you! *Uh, coo, coo-coo-coo!*" he said.

"But . . . I am *not* a papa penguin . . . okay?"

"Squawk, squawk, squawk!" squawked Mama Penguin.

Crack!

"Uh, oh," said Bert. "Not *crack* again!"

The little egg wobbled, and—*crrrrack!*—a baby penguin broke out of the egg.

"Squeak!" said the baby.

"Arf!" added Taxi.

"Squawk!" agreed the mama, hugging her baby. Then she placed the little fellow in Bert's arms.

"Awwww. . ." said Ernie. "Look at that!"

"Come here," said Bert softly. "What a cutie. Heh heh heh. *Coo-coo. Oomf!*"

Mama Penguin stuck a fish in Bert's mouth.

"Oh, how sweet!" said Ernie. "That's the penguin way of thanking you for being such a good papa. I hope you're hungry, ol' buddy. Hee hee hee!"

The End

Love, ELMo

By P.J. Shaw • Illustrated by Tom Brannon

"We're making *mail*," Zoe told Elmo and Abby Cadabby at the park one day.

"Cool!" Elmo said. "What kind of mail?"

"I am drawing a birthday card for *mí abuela*, my grandmother in Mexico," said Rosita.

"And I'm making a thank-you note for my ballet teacher," added Zoe.

"Ooh . . . those are so magical!" exclaimed Abby. "I've never had my very own letter before! Do fairies-in-training get mail?"

"I'm not sure," said Zoe. "But we have crayons and glittery stickers and markers. Want to make one?"

"Thanks, but I have to poof myself home now," said Abby. "My mommy says we're visiting Red Riding Hood's grandmother—or maybe it's the wolf. I can't remember."

"Abby has never ever gotten a letter before," Elmo told his goldfish, Dorothy, that night. "And Abby would like to have a letter of her very own. Wait a minute! Elmo can make a letter for Abby!"

So Elmo found some paper and crayons and asked his mommy for help. Mommy wrote two words at the top:

DEAR ABBY

"What comes next?" Elmo wondered.
"Something from your heart," said Mommy, giving him
a hug. "What do you think would make Abby happy?"

The next day after school, Elmo asked his friends for help.
"What was in Zoe's thank-you note?" Elmo asked Zoe.
"A picture of the Sugar Plum Fairy!" she answered.
"We're learning *The Nutcracker* ballet."

"Can Zoe draw the Sugar Plum Fairy for Abby?"
"Okay!" Zoe said, twirling on her toes. "Abby will love the Sugar Plum Fairy. She wears a fluffy pink tutu and a sparkly tiara!"

"If it's fluffy and sparkly you want, how about a picture of Little Murray Sparkles?" suggested Telly. "She's perfect for a fairy like Abby!"

"Thank you, Telly," said Elmo. "Would Baby Bear like to draw something on Abby's letter, too?"

Boing Boing

"Hmmm . . . I shall draw Cinderella's enchanted carriage," declared Baby Bear, "because Cinderella's fairy godmother created it with a magic spell."

"Good idea!" said Telly. "And how about Cinderella on a pogo stick?"

"Pogo stick?!" asked Elmo.

"Sure," Telly said. "Who wants a carriage when you can *boing* your way to the ball?"

Later that day, Elmo carried Abby's letter to Nani Bird's tree.
"Oh, hello, Elmo," said Big Bird. "We're practicing our hopping.
Now remember, Birdketeers, if you want to get better at something,
it's important to practice. Keep hopping! I'll just stand over here and
be quiet. You won't hear a tweet out of me!"

"Elmo is making a letter for Abby," Elmo explained. "Would Big Bird like to write something?"

"Sure, Elmo. Come on, everybody," Big Bird called. "Let's help write a letter to Abby!"

The Birdketeers drew pictures of daisies, stars, and butterflies—things a fairy might like. And Big Bird wrote a big **A** and **C**.

"**A** is for *Abby* and **C** is for *Cadabby*," he said proudly.

On his way to Bert and Ernie's, Elmo passed Oscar's trash can.
"Can Oscar help make a letter for Abby?" Elmo asked.

"I can, but I won't!" Oscar scowled. "Wait a minute. Maybe if I do,
little Miss Fairy Dust might wave that training wand of hers and fix
my Sloppy Jalopy. Here, gimmee that paper, fur face. Let's see now,
Abby likes pumpkins, right?"

"Ooh, Abby loves pumpkins!" Elmo said.

"Well, this one's nice and *rotten*," Oscar chuckled. "Now scram! I gotta give Slimey his mud bath. And, hey, don't tell anybody I drew that!"

"Okay, Oscar," giggled Elmo. "Have a rotten day!"

"Yeah, yeah," Oscar muttered. "Maybe it'll rain."

"Did I hear someone say *rain*?" asked Super Grover. "That is not good for swirly, adorable superhero capes!"

"Could Super Grover help make a letter for Abby?" Elmo asked.

"A letter? A *letter*? How about the letter **G**?" said Super Grover excitedly. "It has been very useful for this superhero."

And Super Grover scribbled a big, red letter **G**.

"Now, if you will excuse me, I have super-hero deeds to perform and monsters to save," he proclaimed. "Clear the runway! Up, up, and away!"

"Thank you," yelled Elmo. "Super Grover was *super* helpful!"

At 123 Sesame Street, the Twiddlebugs were having a picnic in Bert and Ernie's windowbox.
"Elmo is making a letter for Abby," Elmo said.
"Would Bert and Ernie like to add something?"

"Gee, that sounds like fun, doesn't it, Bert?" asked Ernie. "Let's see, I'll draw a picture of Rubber Duckie and me playing hide and squeak."

"And I'll write down my favorite bird joke," said Bert. "That'll make Abby laugh!"

What's a pigeon's favorite holiday?
Feathers' Day!

When Elmo got to Prairie Dawn's house, everyone was practicing a play for Try-A-New-Food Day.

"Take it from the top!" Prairie shouted. "Oh, Elmo! We really need you to be a mango!"

"Elmo can be a mango tomorrow," Elmo said. "But Elmo is making a letter for Abby today."

"Oh, wait, wait! Me know something to put in letter!" Cookie Monster exclaimed. "It big and round and brown, and it start with letter **C**!"

"Cookie Monster," Prairie sighed. "Everybody *knows* it will be a picture of a cookie!"

"That what you think," said Cookie, drawing . . . a cantaloupe!

"It brown on outside and orange on inside," explained Cookie Monster. "Tasty anytime treat!"

Elmo thought and thought as he walked home on Sesame Street. What could Elmo put in Abby's letter? Abby liked rhyming words— words that sounded the same, like *house* and *mouse* or *play* and *day*. She liked Mother Goose and the Storybook School. . . .

"Greetings!" said Count von Count, appearing suddenly.

"Mr. Count? Elmo has a question," Elmo said. "Elmo wants to put something in a letter to Abby, but how does Elmo pick just one thing?"

"Why would you want to pick just one thing?" asked the Count. "Choose two things, three things, ten things—twenty wonderful things! *Ah ah ah!* Just think of all the possibilities!"

That night, Elmo made up his mind. He drew a special picture on Abby's letter.

Then his daddy helped Elmo write a word at the bottom of the page. Finally Elmo printed his name, nice and s-l-o-w.

And the next day, Abby got her very first letter. She was happy to see all the words and pictures from her friends on Sesame Street. And at the bottom of the page, she read . . .

DEAR ABBY,

A C

G

What is a pigeon's favorite holiday? Feathers' Day

The End